This book belongs to:

TO
THE
WOODS

Read the recipe carefully. Make sure you've got everything you need.

Wash your paws before you start.

Get a grown-up to do the dangerous bits like using sharp knives and working the oven.

Try not to get honey stuck on your whiskers.

YOU WILL NEED:

175g each of self-raising flour, butter or margarine and caster sugar. 3 eggs, 2 tablespoons of milk, jam for filling. Buttercream: 50g butter and 50g icing sugar.

BABY BEAR'S BIRTHDAY CAKE

Set the oven to 190°C, gas mark 5. Grease two 18cm cake tins.

Aaachooo!

1. Beat together the butter and sugar. Gradually add the eggs to the mixture.

2. Add the flour and fold in.

20 mins

3. Spoon the mixture into the cake tins.

5. Let the cakes cool. They should feel springy under your paw.

4. Bake for 20 minutes.

6. Whisk butter and icing sugar together to make buttercream.

7. Sandwich the cakes together using the jam and buttercream.

Save some buttercream for the top.

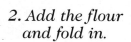

HINTS FOR COOKING ~

Watch your tail so that it doesn't get burnt.

Always use oven gloves when handling hot things.

Don't put your nose straight into the bowl to taste – use a clean spoon.

Don't forget the washing-up.

MUMMY BEAR'S

SANDWICHES

YOU WILL NEED:
bread,
chopping board,
butter,
filling of
your choice,
sharp knife
(to be used by
a grown-up).

1. Butter the bread evenly.

2. Add the filling.

HERE ARE SOME IDEAS

Cheese and tomato

Cucumber mayonnaise and watercress

Peanut butter and jam

Banana and honey

Tomato and basil leaves

3. Cut into quarters.

4. You can use cutters to make sandwich shapes.

5. Arrange on a plate. Serve with crisps and fruit.

For Ramona and Lisa

Mr Wolf can be contacted at **www.hungry-wolf.com**

EGMONT

We bring stories to life

Our story began over a century ago, when seventeen-year-old Egmont Harald Petersen found a coin in the street.
He was on his way to buy a flyswatter, a small hand-operated printing machine that he then set up in his tiny apartment.

The coin brought him such good luck that today Egmont has offices in over 30 countries around the world.
And that lucky coin is still kept at the company's head offices in Denmark.

First published in Great Britain 2001
This edition published 2013
by Egmont UK Limited
The Yellow Building, 1 Nicholas Road, London W11 4AN

Text and illustrations copyright © 2001 Jan Fearnley

Jan Fearnley has asserted her moral rights

ISBN 978 1 4052 1582 4

www.egmont.co.uk

A CIP catalogue record for this title is available from the British Library

Mr Wolf
and the
Three Bears

Jan Fearnley

EGMONT

It was a special day for Mr Wolf. He was feeling very excited, because today his friends the Three Bears were coming round for tea.

It was Baby Bear's birthday, and Mr Wolf was planning a lovely party for everyone.

Mr Wolf wanted to cook a special dish for each one of his guests, and because there was such a lot to do, Grandma came along to help.

"We must be tidy and safe in the kitchen when we're cooking," reminded Grandma. "Let's wash our paws before we start, and then we can have some fun."

For Baby Bear's dish, they looked in the big recipe book.
Soon they found the perfect thing to make.

A birthday cake!

Next they thought about Mummy Bear.
"I know she likes sandwiches," said Mr Wolf.

Grandma remembered there was a recipe in her magazine.

They followed it carefully and soon there was a big heap
of sandwiches on the table, all ready for the party.

Now it was time to make something for
Daddy Bear. Grandma's favourite TV programme
gave them lots of ideas.

"Those Huff Puff cakes sound good,"
said Mr Wolf.

"Good thinking," said Grandma.
"We'd better make lots because
he's a big bear."

They were easy to do.

Then it was Grandma's turn to pick something tasty.
But she couldn't decide what she wanted.

Mr Wolf had a brainwave.

Mr Wolf helped Grandma look on the internet for
some ideas. At www.hungry-wolf.com Grandma found
a recipe she fancied – Cheesy Snipsnaps!

They printed out the recipe and set to work.

Mr Wolf and Grandma still had a lot to do before their guests arrived.

They blew up balloons,

wrapped Baby Bear's present,

laid the table

and made some party hats.

Grandma arranged some flowers.

Then they tidied the house from top . . .

to bottom . . . .

until it looked lovely.

"Ready!" said Mr Wolf, just as they heard a knock on the door.

"Come in! Welcome!" cried Mr Wolf.
"Happy Birthday, Baby Bear!"

But somebody came barging in before them!

IT WAS GOLDILOCKS!

"Let me come in, Mr Wolf," she demanded.
"I smell nice things a-cooking."
"What have you brought her for?"
whispered Mr Wolf. "She always causes trouble."

"She followed us through the woods," said Daddy Bear.
"There was nothing we could do! She said she was
invited too."

"What a fibber!" said Mr Wolf.

"Don't be mean! Let the child come in," called Grandma
from her chair. "But you'd better behave yourself,
Goldilocks," she warned.

"Yeah, yeah," shrugged Goldilocks, tossing her curls.
"I promise."

But it wasn't long before Goldilocks forgot her promise.

When they were dancing, she trod on Mr Wolf's toe
and didn't say sorry.

When they played pass the parcel, Goldilocks took off
all the wrappers instead of just one.

When they played musical chairs,
Goldilocks was too rough – and she cheated!

Grandma didn't join in the games. She just sat in her chair,
as grandmas often do, watching.
"I think it's time for tea," she said. But . . .

. . . someone had got there first!

"Somebody's had a bite out of this cake," said Daddy Bear.
"Somebody's been at this sandwich, too," said Mummy Bear.
"Mine's nearly all gone!" cried Baby Bear.
"This always happens to me!"

"Your food's yukky," complained Goldilocks, with her cheeks bulging. Her table manners were atrocious!
Poor Mr Wolf. "My party is a disaster!" he whimpered.
Grandma smiled at Mr Wolf and slowly got to her feet.
"It's time for another game," she said.

"Let's play hide and seek."
"Boring," said Goldilocks.
"I always win."
"We'll see," said Grandma.

Everyone ran off to hide.
Grandma counted to one
hundred. "Coming! Ready
or not!" she called.

She took a while . . .

. . . but she did find
everybody eventually . . .

. . . that is, all except
for Goldilocks.
She was nowhere to be seen.

"What a rude girl," said Mummy Bear. "She nearly
ruined our party and now she's gone off without
saying thank you."
"Never mind," said Grandma. "I've got a surprise."
She disappeared into the kitchen . . .

. . . and emerged with a beautiful great big pie,
all steaming hot from the oven, with a golden,
melt-in-the-mouth crumbly pastry crust.

"Clever Grandma!" everybody cheered.

"Let's gobble it up while it's hot!" said Mr Wolf.
"Not just yet," said Grandma.
"I think this is a dish best served cold."

And as they waited for the golden pie to cool,
Grandma giggled to herself and settled back
to enjoy the rest of the party.

"Save me a big piece," she said,
". . . a very big piece.
I'm starving!"

DADDY BEAR'S HUFF PUFFS

YOU WILL NEED:

175g chocolate, 50g butter,
2 tablespoons syrup,
125g rice crispies, cornflakes or huff puffs,
paper cake cases.

1. Put butter and syrup into pan.

2. Add the chocolate. Save some for the pan please, Grandma.

3. Heat gently until melted.

4. Add the crispies and mix together.

5. Carefully spoon into cases. Allow to cool, then put in the fridge to harden.

*Don't balance them on your nose.
It's not polite!*

YOU WILL NEED:

125g self raising flour,
pinch salt, 1/2 teaspoon
of mustard powder,
50g butter,
75g grated cheese, 1 egg

1. Sieve the flour, salt and mustard into a bowl.

3. Roll out dough on a floured surface until quite thin. Use cutters or a knife to make shapes.

5. Cool on a wire rack. They taste great on the day but will also keep in a tin for a few days.

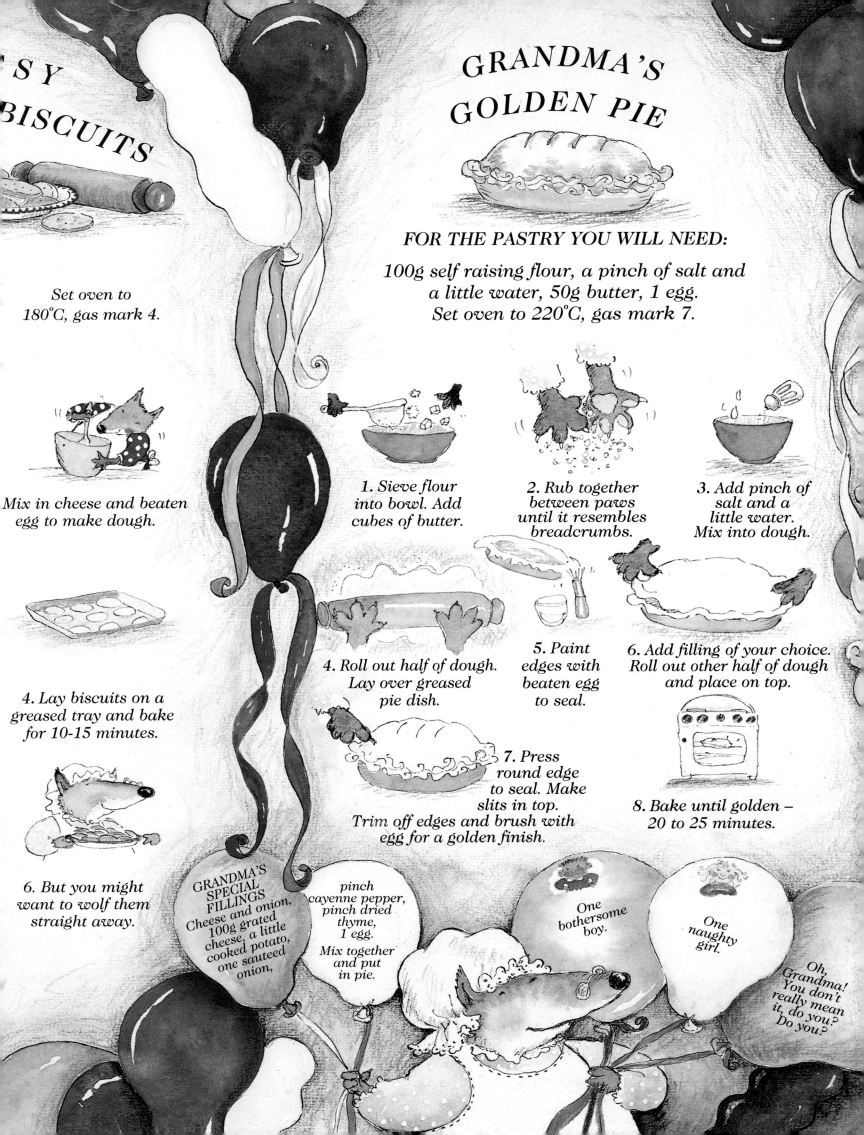

SY BISCUITS

Set oven to 180°C, gas mark 4.

Mix in cheese and beaten egg to make dough.

4. Lay biscuits on a greased tray and bake for 10-15 minutes.

6. But you might want to wolf them straight away.

GRANDMA'S GOLDEN PIE

FOR THE PASTRY YOU WILL NEED:

100g self raising flour, a pinch of salt and a little water, 50g butter, 1 egg.
Set oven to 220°C, gas mark 7.

1. Sieve flour into bowl. Add cubes of butter.

2. Rub together between paws until it resembles breadcrumbs.

3. Add pinch of salt and a little water. Mix into dough.

4. Roll out half of dough. Lay over greased pie dish.

5. Paint edges with beaten egg to seal.

6. Add filling of your choice. Roll out other half of dough and place on top.

7. Press round edge to seal. Make slits in top. Trim off edges and brush with egg for a golden finish.

8. Bake until golden – 20 to 25 minutes.

GRANDMA'S SPECIAL FILLINGS
Cheese and onion, 100g grated cheese, a little cooked potato, one sauteed onion, pinch cayenne pepper, pinch dried thyme, 1 egg. Mix together and put in pie.

One bothersome boy.

One naughty girl.

Oh, Grandma! You don't really mean it, do you? Do you?